A Picture

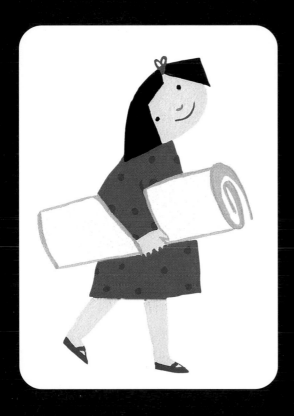

written by Mary Evans
illustrated by Lizi Boyd

**McGraw-Hill
School Division**

New York   Farmington

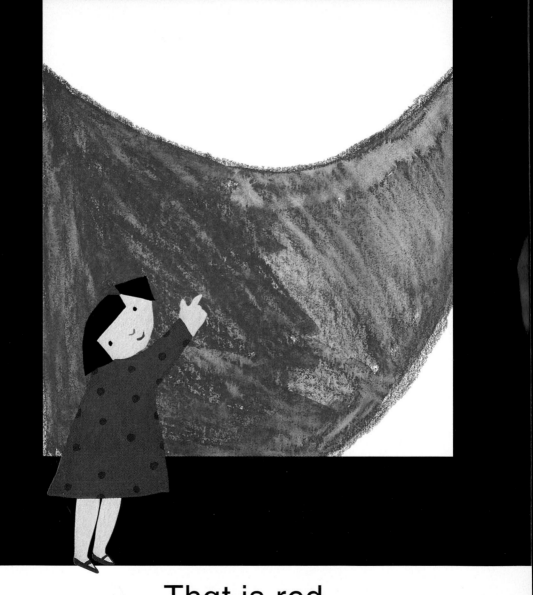

That is red.

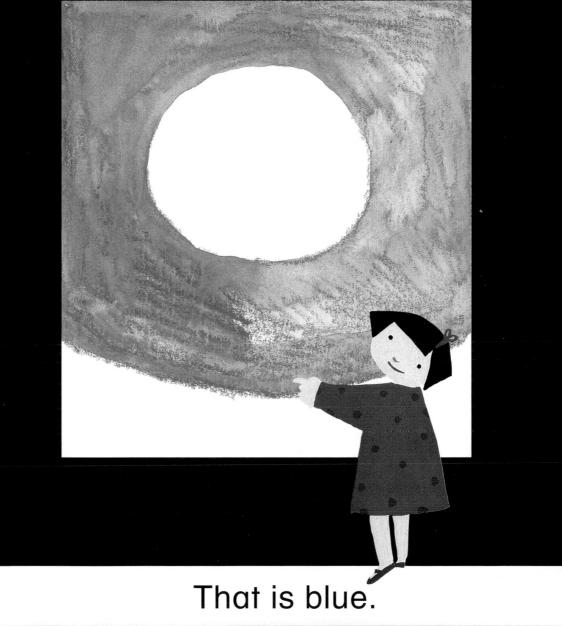

That is blue.

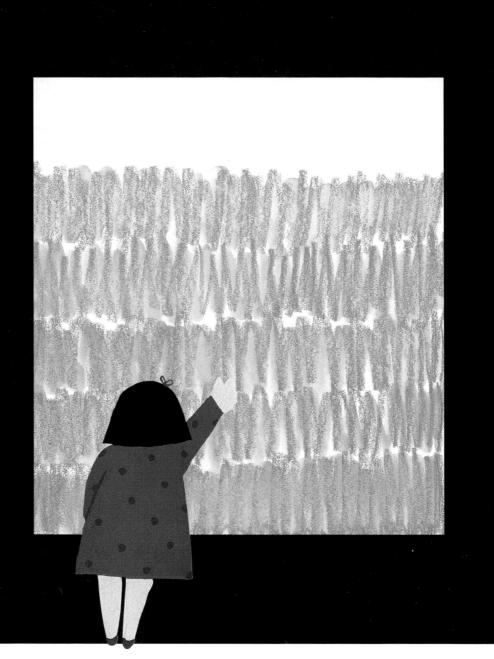

That is green.

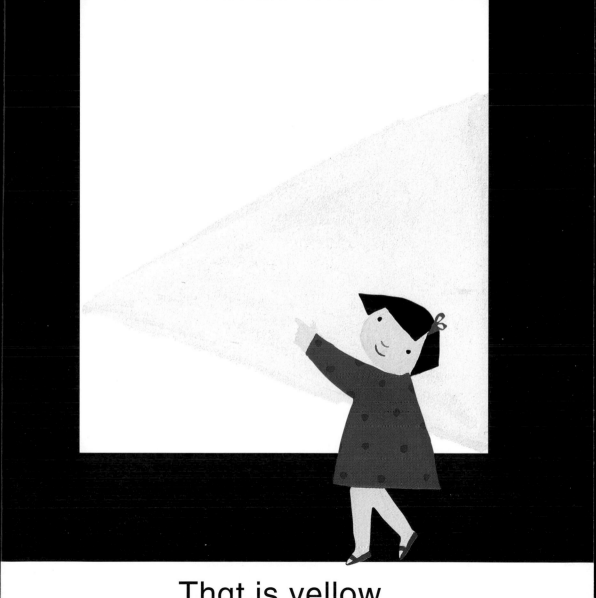

That is yellow.

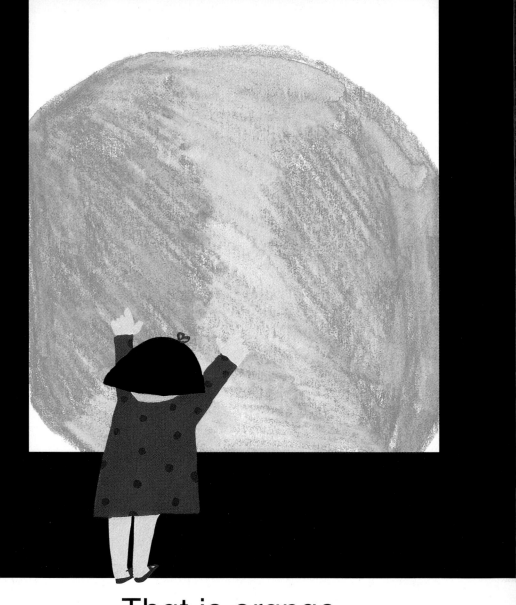

That is orange.

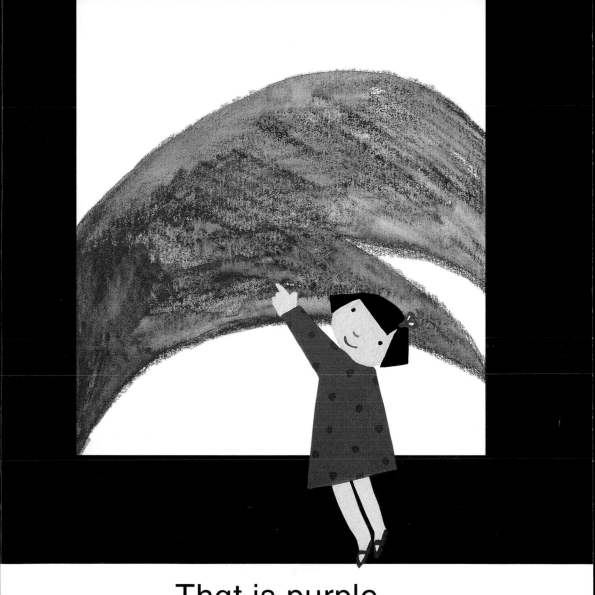

That is purple.

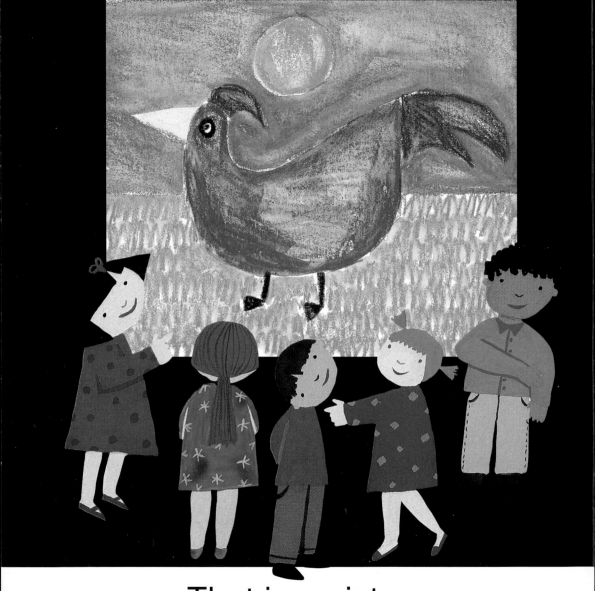

That is a picture.